ISBN 0-8114-9320-2

4 5 6 7 8 9 01 00 99

Produced by Mega-Books of New York, Inc.
Design and Art Direction by Michaelis/Carpelis Design Assoc.

Cover illustration: Tom Roberts

Behind the Screams

by Ann Weil

interior illustrations by
Keith Neely

STECK-VAUGHN
C O M P A N Y

CHAPTER ONE

"Are you sure this is where the flyer said we should come?" Julio Cruz asked his friends. He scanned the deserted streets and empty warehouses. "This doesn't seem like a place where someone would want to make a science fiction movie."

Molly Eng read the flyer she held in her hand. "It says right here, the corner of West Street and Cleveland Avenue."

"Look over there," cried Peter Kramer. He pointed to a large silver structure a couple of blocks away. "That must be it!"

The three teenagers walked quickly toward the structure. They each tried to act cool, but deep down inside they were excited about the idea of being in a science fiction movie filmed in their own hometown.

Molly had seen the flyer at Stellar Burgers the previous night. She and her friends met at the diner every Friday after school to make plans for the weekend.

The flyer was posted next to the pay phones behind Molly's regular booth. The carefully drawn spaceship had immediately caught Molly's eye.

Molly was a big science fiction film fan. She had seen *Jupiter Jo* so many times she knew every line of the script by heart. And she had bought all three videotapes of the *Moon Warrior* trilogy with money she had saved from babysitting.

When Molly had gotten up from the booth and taken a closer look at the flyer, the words "Vandroid Productions" leaped out at her. The name was printed in big block letters across the top of the flyer. Underneath, in smaller letters, was a notice:

VANDROID PRODUCTIONS

WANTED:
TEENAGERS TO WORK AS EXTRAS IN A SCIENCE FICTION MOVIE.
APPLY IN PERSON,
SATURDAY MORNING, 7 AM

Molly took the flyer with her when she and her friends left Stellar Burgers. She tried to get the others excited about the idea of being a movie extra. But most of them didn't think it was worth getting up at dawn on a Saturday morning and traveling to the far side of town.

"Sure," Molly had admitted to herself, "it's probably some low-budget movie with a bunch of no-name actors, and sets that look like a high school class threw them together for their student play, but . . ."

But Molly was a die-hard movie buff who didn't care if she recognized any of the actors' names. She just wanted to get behind the scenes of a real movie with a director, a technical crew, costumes, makeup, and everything else that went into the magic of making movies, even bad movies!

Molly wasn't surprised when Julio Cruz had agreed to go with her. Julio was the president of the science fiction club at school. He wouldn't miss this chance to meet some "aliens," even if they were only make-believe.

And Peter Kramer, Julio's best friend—well, he hadn't had anything better to do that Saturday morning.

So Molly, Peter, and Julio had all set their alarm clocks to meet up in the middle of town and arrive together in time for casting.

It was just a few minutes before 7:00 a.m. when they reached the large grassy corner lot.

The three teens glanced at each other in amazement.

"Wow!" said Julio, gazing at the large spaceship-like set in front of them.

The silvery material shone like a mirror. From a distance, the spaceship blended in with the industrial surroundings as if it were just another one of the newer buildings. If the three teens hadn't been looking specifically for the movie set, they would have missed it altogether.

"This looks exactly like the picture on the flyer," said Molly.

Several tough-looking men were standing stiffly around the spaceship. Molly guessed that they were part of the movie crew.

She walked up to one of them. "Excuse me," Molly said. "We, uh, saw this flyer, and so we're here to try out for the movie. We want to be extras."

The man looked at the flyer. Then he pointed toward a big sign on the other side of the lot. It said: VANDROID PRODUCTIONS. ACTORS/EXTRAS SIGN IN HERE.

"Thank you," said Molly. She and Peter and Julio headed toward the sign.

"That's what I call a man of few words," joked Peter.

As they crossed the lot, Julio noticed that several of the actors were already in costume. The "aliens" in this movie were tall. The shortest was six feet. They were all very thin and completely covered in brightly colored fur, even their faces. The aliens' eyes were

a very bright yellow.

"Wow! Those costumes are great!" said Julio. He started to walk toward the furry beings.

Peter tugged him on the arm. "What are you doing? We have to go sign in," Peter urged.

"I just wanted to get a closer look," Julio answered.

"Come on," urged Molly to both her friends. She looked at her watch. "It's already seven. I don't want to lose our chance to be cast as extras just because you two are goofing around."

"Okay," said Julio reluctantly. "I guess I can check them out later."

"Don't you think those guys look kind of like Moki from the *Moon Warrior* movies?" Peter asked.

"Yeah, they do," said Molly, thinking about her beloved trilogy. "Hey, maybe I'll get to dress up like Queen Zora of Planet Jupiter," she added, wrapping an imaginary cloak around her shoulders.

They were just coming to the sign-in area when a strange-looking man in dark sunglasses and a baseball cap approached them. "Hello," he said in a hoarse voice. "I'm Neil Lambert, the director. You must be here to try out for our movie."

"Yes," Molly answered for all three teens. "We saw the flyer and . . ."

"Good, good, good," interrupted Neil. He adjusted the bandana around his neck. When he spoke again, his voice sounded much clearer. "If you'll just sign these release forms we can get to work."

Neil handed each of the teens a sheet of paper with only one short paragraph typed on it:

I ,_____(your name here), hereby surrender control of my mind and body to Vandroid Productions.

_____
(your signature)
_____, 2050
(date)

"That's pretty funny," said Peter as he started to sign the paper.

"What are you doing?" hissed Julio. "You're not really going to give them control of your mind and body, are you?"

"Of course not," said Peter. "This is just some kind of joke. They'll probably use it for publicity or something."

"Yeah," Molly added. "I mean, how could they take control of our minds and bodies anyway?" She signed her copy as well.

"Okay, I guess I'm in, too," said Julio as he signed his copy.

I, _____
(YOUR NAME HERE)
HERE BY SURRENDER
CONTROL OF MY MIND
AND BODY TO VANDROID
PRODUCTIONS.

_____
(YOUR SIGNATURE)
_____, 2050
(DATE)

CHAPTER TWO

Neil Lambert snatched the signed forms from the teenagers' hands. "Excellent!" he exclaimed. "Now, please follow me."

He led them past clusters of hi-tech equipment to another corner of the lot. There, Neil stopped to talk with a thin woman with wild frizzy hair. She had on a shiny pink jumpsuit and oversized black boots.

Molly admired what the woman was wearing. She had never seen anything like the material the jumpsuit was made from. The boots were definitely weird. But the whole effect was very cool.

The woman started mixing a large pot

of white paste. Next to her, a long table held all sorts of odds and ends. Some things were brightly colored and sparkled in the morning sun.

"Hmmm, this must be the makeup department," Molly said to her friends.

"I don't know," said Julio. "The other actors have pretty complicated costumes. That fur looks so real. And how do they get those yellow eyes? They must be wearing yellow contact lenses," he reasoned. "There's got to be a separate special effects department somewhere around here, too."

"Hey," said Molly, glancing around without responding to Julio. "Where's Peter?"

Julio turned around to look for his friend. There were only a dozen or so people on the lot. Half of them were in the alien costumes. "There he is," Julio said, pointing. "He's talking to that woman."

Molly looked where Julio was pointing and spotted Peter talking to a beautiful woman in a shiny gold costume. "That's Suzanne Moore!" exclaimed Molly. "She was on that TV series, *No One's Home*."

"Molly," interrupted Neil. She had

forgotten the director in the midst of her stargazing. "This is Jana. She will take care of you now." With that, Neil quickly walked away.

Jana looked up briefly, then continued mixing the paste.

"Hi," said Molly. She looked around and was surprised there was no mirror. She thought all makeup people

used lighted mirrors.

Jana's mouth stretched into a smile, but she didn't say anything. She motioned toward the chair next to the table, and Molly sat down. Jana immediately spread a thick layer of the pasty stuff all over Molly's face.

At first Molly panicked when Jana covered her mouth and nose. But surprisingly, Molly found she could breathe easily through the thick white goo. It felt like melted marshmallows and smelled like dirt.

"If this is the glamour of Hollywood," Molly thought, "I'll stick to high school."

After about thirty seconds, Jana peeled the stuff off of Molly's face. It came away in one rubbery piece.

Molly slowly opened her eyes and watched as Jana flipped the white mold inside out. Molly couldn't believe what she saw. Jana was holding a perfect likeness of her face!

"How did you do that?" Molly asked in amazement. The hardened paste had even picked up her skin tone. It was an exact match. Even the small mole on Molly's neck was in precisely the right spot.

But Jana didn't answer Molly's question. She was busy with her work.

Molly reached out to touch the mask, but Jana whisked it out of her reach.

"Sorry," Molly apologized. "I was just wondering what it was made from." She paused a moment, but Jana still didn't say anything.

"Well, I guess if you're done, I'll go find my friends," Molly said. She hesitated, waiting for any response from Jana. But Jana was busy preparing more paste.

After a more few seconds of uncomfortable silence, Molly got up from the chair and left.

Molly knew that Hollywood had pretty great special effects. But she never imagined that they could do such fine work so quickly.

"Jana must be one of the best in her field," Molly thought as she looked around for Peter and Julio. Still, she was more than a little disappointed that Jana hadn't been more talkative. Molly wondered what they would use the mask of her face for in the movie.

She pulled herself out of her thoughts when she found Peter still talking with Suzanne Moore.

"Hi," Molly said to Peter. She smiled shyly at Suzanne. Molly had never met a TV star before. She didn't know what to say. Then Molly noticed that the beautiful actress was wearing a large pendant. It was tied snugly around her neck with a thick piece of ribbon. It was unlike anything Molly had ever seen. "I love your necklace!" Molly exclaimed.

"Thank you," Suzanne said in a deep, husky voice.

"So, uh, Ms. Moore, could you maybe

tell us about the movie's plot?" Molly asked, trying to make conversation.

Suzanne smiled. "There isn't really a plot. Neil likes us to improvise. You know, make it up as we go along."

"What about the aliens?" asked Peter. "Do they try to kill all the Earthlings and take over the planet?"

Suzanne's amber eyes shone with amusement. "No, the Vandroids have a perfectly fine planet of their own. Vandra is much larger than Earth, and the Vandroids have just about everything they need."

"Then why do the Vandroids come to Earth?" asked Molly.

"You'll find out when Neil calls you for your scene. He likes his extras to be surprised. Their looks are more natural that way."

"Hey!" Julio called out to his friends as he jogged over to them. "Jana just made a really cool cast of my head."

"She did mine, too," replied Molly.

"She's pretty amazing, isn't she?"

"Excuse me," Suzanne whispered, and she wandered away in the direction of the spaceship. Peter sighed heavily.

"I guess a famous TV star like Suzanne Moore has better things to do than talk to us," joked Julio.

"Hey, just because she's on TV doesn't mean she's a snob," Peter said. He had a dazed look in his eyes as he watched Suzanne stroll across the lot.

"Starstruck so soon?" Molly teased her friend.

"Get a grip, Peter. It's your turn to get slimed," Julio said. He nodded in Jana's direction. "She's waiting for you."

Peter was still thinking about Suzanne Moore as he walked over to Jana's table.

"What now?" Molly asked Julio.

"Let's go find Neil," Julio suggested. "He's probably at the spaceship. I want to check the set out anyway."

Molly and Julio approached the spaceship, which was about the size of a house. It was shaped like a diamond and supported on stilt-like legs.

"It's so beautiful!" said Molly as she gazed up at the huge gleaming jewel.

"Don't look now, but I think we're being followed," Julio whispered, pointing behind him. Four members of the crew were walking toward them.

"Oh, don't be so paranoid," said Molly. "Come on, let's look for Neil."

They walked all around the set, trying to find a way in. But there did not seem to be any entrance.

"That's weird," said Julio. "Usually there's a big open space so the cameras can move around to film the scene."

Just then the crew members appeared from the other side of the spaceship. With serious looks on their faces, they walked straight toward Molly and Julio.

"Uh-oh, something tells me we're not supposed to be on this set," Molly said nervously.

But before Molly and Julio could move, they were surrounded.

CHAPTER THREE

"Hi," Julio said. His voice cracked with fear. The men didn't smile or return his greeting.

"Have you seen Neil?" asked Molly, trying to sound casual as the men took both of them by the arms. They lifted Molly and Julio off the ground and carried them away from the spaceship.

"Oh, here you are," croaked Neil. The director had appeared from nowhere. He nodded at the men. They released Molly and Julio and walked back toward the spaceship. "I forgot to mention one thing earlier," Neil said. "The spaceship is off-limits to hu—, I mean extras. The workers are still touching up the scenery. I wanted some last minute changes. We'll be ready for your scene after breakfast."

Before Molly and Julio could ask what their scene was about, Neil whisked them over to a long table covered with food.

"Have something to eat," Neil offered. "I'll send someone to get you when we're ready." Neil adjusted his bandana and left.

Peter was already at one end of the table. He was digging away at a stack of pancakes and gulping down a big glass of chocolate milk.

"D-lishous!" he said through a mouthful of food.

Julio and Molly helped themselves. The three of them were the only ones going for the pancakes and chocolate milk. The rest of the actors and crew were huddled at the other end of the table holding bowls of what looked like steaming soup.

"What are they eating?" Julio asked Peter. He pointed toward the others who were noisily sucking up the soup through large straws.

"I don't know," said Peter. "But I don't think I want to find out. I got a whiff of it, and it smelled like gasoline. Whew!"

"It's probably some new Hollywood diet," said Molly, sipping her chocolate milk. "I heard that actors have strange eating habits."

"That's for sure," said Julio. He wiped some syrup off his chin. "I don't see how they can eat anything through all that furry makeup anyhow."

"That's probably why they're using straws . . . and why they're all so skinny," suggested Molly.

Just as the teens finished their breakfast, one of the crew members approached them. He gestured sternly for the teens to follow him.

"Another big talker," remarked Peter.

The man led them to a small booth and pointed to a sign with instructions. It read:

Step inside one at a time. State your full name, age, parents' names, address, telephone number, and your favorite foods. Make sure to speak slowly and clearly.

Their silent guide then left them there to do as instructed.

"What do you think that's for?" Peter asked Julio as Molly entered the booth.

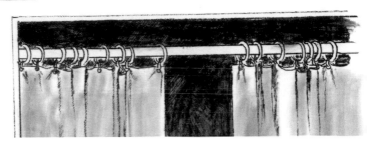

STEP INSIDE ONE AT A TIME.
STATE YOUR FULL NAME, AGE,
PARENTS' NAMES, ADDRESS,
TELEPHONE NUMBER, AND
YOUR FAVORITE FOODS.
MAKE SURE TO SPEAK
SLOWLY AND CLEARLY.

"I guess it's some kind of sound check," answered Julio.

After Molly came out, Peter went in. A few minutes later, Julio took his turn.

"I see everything's going as planned," said Neil, rushing over to the booth just as Julio stepped out. Behind Neil a crew member was holding what looked like a small camera.

"We need some pictures of you three," said Neil. He positioned Julio, Molly

33

and Peter a few yards apart so that the camera operator could walk around each of them. The machine in his hand hummed softly.

"What kind of camera are you using?" Julio asked.

"It's a holographic camera," explained Neil. "We're using it to take a complete three-dimensional image of each of you."

Molly was about to ask why they

needed three-dimensional pictures of extras, but Neil interrupted her thoughts.

"So, Molly, do you have any hobbies?" he asked as the camera rolled.

"Well, I like to ski," she answered.

"How about you, Julio?" Neil continued.

"I like to design stuff on my computer," Julio said.

"And you, Peter?" Neil asked.

"Fishing, I guess," Peter answered. "And basketball."

"Good, good, good," said Neil as he hurried away toward the spaceship.

"What was that about?" Molly whispered.

"Maybe Neil's just being friendly. You know, making conversation," Peter said.

"That's more than can be said for the others around here," Molly noted, watching the camera operator walk around Julio.

The machine stopped humming and the camera operator marched back to the spaceship.

"Let's go after Neil and get a script," suggested Julio. "I want to see what this movie is all about."

"He was headed toward the spaceship," said Molly.

"Then let's go!" Julio started for the spaceship.

"Are you coming?" Molly asked Peter.

"No," Peter answered. "I think I'll just

hang out here for a bit."

Molly noticed Suzanne Moore coming their way. Her gold costume shimmered. "See if you can get an autographed picture for me, too," Molly said with a smile.

"Oh yeah, sure," mumbled Peter as he walked toward the beautiful TV star.

Molly rolled her eyes. "That boy!" Then she hurried to catch up to Julio.

CHAPTER FOUR

Molly caught up with Julio at the base of the spaceship set. He was looking at one of the stilt-like supports.

"What are you doing?" asked Molly.

Julio tapped the silver support with his fingernail. It made no sound. "I was just wondering what it's made of," Julio said as he ran his hand over the spaceship's surface. "It's definitely not wood or metal. It must be some kind of weird plastic."

Molly looked around nervously. "Well, whatever it is, it's off-limits, remember?" she said.

"I think I've found it," Julio said as he traced his fingers lightly over the

smooth, shiny surface.

"Found what?" asked Molly.

"This!" Julio pressed the palm of his hand against a dip in the ship's exterior. Immediately, a long ladder came out of the side of the ship. It slid soundlessly down to the ground a few feet from where Julio and Molly stood.

"Wow, this is some movie set!" said Molly.

Julio looked thoughtful. "I'm beginning to wonder if this is a set at all," he said quietly.

"What do you mean?" asked Molly.

"I know it sounds crazy, but before Jana did my face, I snuck around and examined some of the equipment that's out on the lot. It doesn't look like any movie equipment I've ever seen."

"And how much professional movie equipment *have* you seen?" asked Molly.

"Well, none actually," admitted Julio. "But I've seen some on TV."

"So what do you think is really going on?" Molly asked, humoring her friend.

"I don't think this spaceship is a set for a movie," said Julio. "I think it's a real alien spaceship."

"Right," Molly wisecracked. "And the Vandroids aren't just a bunch of actors in furry costumes. They're real aliens

from another planet."

"Yes. That's exactly what I think," said Julio seriously.

Molly laughed. "Look, Julio, I like science fiction, too. But I don't confuse it with reality."

"Think about it, Molly," Julio responded. "Making masks of our faces, taking 3-D pictures, recording our voices. . . it's like they want to be able to impersonate us somehow."

As he spoke, Julio became more and more persuasive. "Neil could be wearing one of Jana's masks over his real Vandroid face. And have you noticed the way he's always adjusting that bandana around his neck? I think it's hiding some kind of voice simulator."

"Now that you mention it, I did notice a strange pendant around Suzanne Moore's neck," Molly said. "Maybe that's why Suzanne and Neil are the only ones who have spoken to us. But even if they are from another planet—and I'm not convinced they are—what are we supposed to do?"

"We can't just go tell someone here, that's for sure," said Julio. "No one would believe us. And by the time we convinced them we weren't totally nuts, Vandroid Productions would probably be on their way to another solar system."

Julio scratched his head as if that would help him come up with a good

idea. "I think we should check out the spaceship," he suggested. "If I'm right, and the Vandroids really are from outer space, we'll find Peter, get out of here, and report this. If I'm wrong, Neil will probably just yell at us for being on the set again."

Molly wasn't so sure it was that simple.

"Are you coming?" asked Julio as he started to climb the ladder.

Molly looked around. Most of the crew were still eating breakfast. No one seemed to be watching the spaceship. Molly followed Julio up the ladder and into the spaceship.

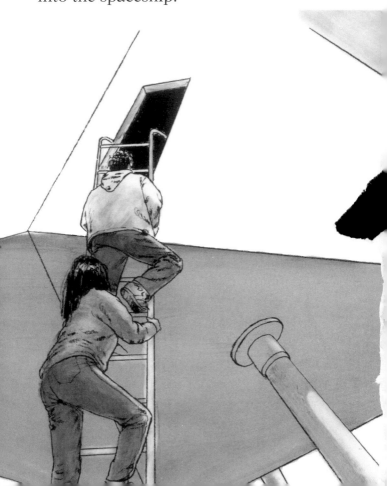

CHAPTER FIVE

Molly expected the rugged crew members to appear at any moment and toss them out of the spaceship . . . or worse! But Julio seemed right at home in the strange surroundings.

The corridor where Molly and Julio stood was shaped like a cylinder. There were no ceilings, walls or floors. All of the spaceship's surfaces blended into one another, like the inside of a giant silver tube.

Molly and Julio's reflections were slightly distorted in the smooth, shiny material, as they would be in a fun house mirror.

But Molly didn't feel like she was at a

carnival. This was like a nightmare.

For a moment she thought about turning around and running back out. But she couldn't leave Julio alone in the spaceship. "If this really is dangerous," she thought to herself, "we've got to stick together."

Molly slid her hand over the inside surface of the spaceship, expecting it to feel cold and hard. Instead, the surface felt soft and warm, almost as if it were alive. Molly shuddered and quickly pulled her hand away from the surface.

Julio had rushed ahead. "Over here," he whispered, motioning for Molly to come join him.

Molly took a deep breath to calm herself. She walked up to where Julio was standing.

The corridor opened up into a small room. One wall was lined with shelves. "Look!" Julio pointed to some shelves full of masks. On the middle shelf were some very familiar faces. Julio and

Molly were staring right into their own eyes!

And right above their masks was one of Peter, too. On another shelf were masks like the faces of the men who had

hauled them away from the spaceship an hour before.

Hanging on a pole near the shelves were a variety of different colored jumpsuits.

"This is perfect!" cried Julio, thumbing through the jumpsuits and taking things off the shelves.

"What do you mean?" asked Molly.

"We can disguise ourselves in these costumes and explore the ship without getting caught," Julio said. He pulled a man's mask over his head.

"Do you really think this will work?" Molly asked.

"It worked in the third *Moon Warrior* movie," Julio said. "Remember when Kelly Running-Star and Matt Uno disguised themselves to rescue Queen Zora from Nalla Derga?" Julio pulled a jumpsuit on over his clothes as he reminded Molly of her favorite characters' heroic actions.

But before she could say anything,

Molly heard approaching footsteps. She quickly slipped on a jumpsuit and mask. "Someone's coming!" Molly whispered.

"Just don't say anything," warned Julio as he turned around.

Two furry Vandroids were just a few yards away. Molly felt sweaty

underneath her mask. She wasn't sure if it was because she believed that the Vandroids really were aliens, or if she was just afraid of getting caught in an area where she wasn't supposed to be.

The Vandroids walked right by without even stopping. When they had passed, Molly let out a sigh of relief. "That was close," she said.

Julio nodded and put his finger to his lips. Then they hurried down the corridor to check out the rest of the spaceship.

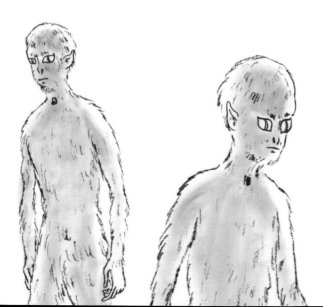

CHAPTER SIX

"So what do you do for fun?" asked Suzanne Moore.

Peter blushed. He couldn't believe Suzanne Moore was actually interested in a regular nobody like himself.

"Well, actually," he began, "I'm a professional race car driver."

"Really?" Suzanne smiled.

"Yeah, you know, rocket car racing, stuff like that." Peter hoped hi would impress Suzanne Moore. Maybe she would even go out with him after they finished shooting the movie! He'd make sure to take her where all his friends could see them together.

Suzanne leaned in so close to Peter's

face, he thought she was going to kiss him. He closed his eyes.

"Peter?" she said softly.

"Yes?" he answered breathlessly.

"Would you like to go to the spaceship with me? You could help me rehearse."

"Oh, sure," said Peter, opening his eyes. He was disappointed that she hadn't kissed him. But maybe he'd have another opportunity. He eagerly followed her to the spaceship.

Back at the spaceship, Julio and Molly had covered a lot of ground.

"Now do you believe me?" asked Julio as he and Molly entered a room off the end of the corridor. So far, they hadn't seen a single sign of a movie being made. And it was clear that the spaceship was not designed as a set.

Molly couldn't deny it any longer. She nodded, feeling numb all over. She barely noticed the live mice, rabbits, and other small creatures in cages lining one wall of the room.

"These tables are kind of like the ones in biology lab at school," Julio said, bringing Molly's thoughts back to the spaceship room.

Molly picked up a strange-looking tool from one of the tables. It was long and sharp. She glanced over at the caged animals. "Do you think the Vandroids use these to . . ." Molly couldn't finish her sentence. The thought was too horrible.

Julio was thinking the same thing, but even worse. "What if they're planning to put *us* in cages?" He felt faint. "We've got to find Peter and get out of here," Julio cried.

Molly hesitated for a second. Then she quickly flipped up the clasps on the

tried to act like a Vandroid as she passed the real aliens.

She had almost caught up with Julio when she felt a pair of furry arms wrap around her from behind. Molly was practically lifted off the ground.

"Run, Julio!" Molly shouted. Julio started to bolt—but he ran smack into Neil Lambert. The director quickly grabbed the boy.

"Clever disguises," Neil snarled as he ripped off Julio's mask. Then the director pulled off his own mask and his bandana. There was a small box resting against his throat. Neil's next words seemed to come directly from that box.

"Clever, clever, you humans are indeed. But you forgot about your sneakers." He pointed at Julio's and Molly's feet. "We don't have footware like that back on Vandra."

"Let us go!" Julio growled as he struggled to get loose.

With his free hand, Neil waved the

release forms in front of Julio's face. "You've already given us control of your mind and body," the Vandroid sneered. "So we can do whatever we want with you."

"Don't be ridiculous. Those forms are meaningless!" protested Molly as she twisted in the arms of another Vandroid.

"Not on Vandra, they're not," argued Neil. He took Molly's mask as well. "They're just what we need to do what we've planned. Your papers are all in order to show the Vandroid authorities."

"What are you going to do with us?" asked Julio angrily.

"You'll find out soon enough," Neil answered.

The Vandroids took Molly and Julio to a small room filled with TV monitors.

"Wait here," said Neil. "Relax. Watch TV. You can get all your Earth stations. Or you can see what's going on elsewhere in the spaceship, since you

seem to be so interested. Have fun!"
Neil gave a wicked laugh. "I'll be back
for you in a few minutes." The director
left and slammed the door behind him.
The teenagers heard the sound of a lock
falling into place.

Julio immediately started to fiddle
with the TV monitors.

"I can't believe you're going to watch
television at a time like this!" cried
Molly.

Julio picked up a small gadget with lots of buttons on it. "This looks like some kind of remote control," he said. He started hitting some of the buttons. "Neil got one thing right. I *do* want to see what's going on around here."

Different images flashed on the monitors all around the room as Julio pushed the buttons.

"Hey, there's Peter!" shouted Molly, pointing to one of the screens. "Suzanne's got him!"

Julio hit another button on the remote control and suddenly they could hear what Peter and Suzanne were saying.

"What scene will they be filming in here?" asked Peter. Suzanne had led him inside a large room filled with plants, flowers and trees. It was like a greenhouse. A fishing pole lay on the ground next to a small pond stocked with brightly colored fish. A small basketball court looked out of place,

tucked into one corner of the room.

"This is your new home," said Suzanne calmly. "When we get back to Vandra, you will become a major attraction for our people. Vandroids are eager to find out about life on Planet Earth. They have seen replicas of plants and animals, even replicas of human beings like yourself. But they have never actually seen real *live* Earth beings. It will be a great moment when our expedition returns with our human specimens."

"Boy, you sure play your part well!" Peter said in a flattering tone of voice. "And it's great how you can recite your lines so easily. I always wanted to know how actors managed to memorize all that stuff."

"Oh, I'm not reciting anything," said Suzanne. She turned her back to Peter. "I'm telling you the truth. You will be part of the greatest exhibit on Vandra."

The meaning of Suzanne's words

didn't hit Peter immediately. But when the actress turned around to face him, Peter gasped in horror.

Suzanne had pulled off her human mask. Peter was staring right into the bright yellow eyes of a furry faced Vandroid!

CHAPTER SEVEN

"Okay," said Peter, trying to remain calm. "I admit, I fell for it." He started walking around the room, looking up, down, and sideways.

"Where are the hidden cameras, Neil?" Peter called out. "I hope you got my expression, because I don't think I could fake that for a second take." Peter waited for the director to appear.

"There is no movie, Peter." Suzanne's deep, husky voice sounded strange coming from the Vandroid's throat. "We wanted a few teenage humans to take back to Vandra, so we put up that flyer at the restaurant. We thought young people eager to be in a science fiction movie would be easy to control, especially if they saw some familiar TV stars on the set."

Peter stared in disbelief.

"We've made replicas of you and your friends to leave behind here on Earth," Suzanne continued. "No one will miss you until we are safely back on Vandra."

Peter was stunned. Could Suzanne's words be true? Was Vandroid Productions just a cover? Could these really be extra-terrestrials who were here to take back samples of Earth life for some kind of outer space theme park?

"You can't make us be in your amusement park! I don't want to be a zoo animal for Vandroids!" yelled Peter.

"You won't feel that way for long," said Suzanne. She pulled out a weapon that resembled a large plastic water pistol. "Don't be scared," added Suzanne. "This won't hurt a bit."

"Oh, no!" cried Molly, watching the

scene on the monitors. "She's going to kill him!"

Just as a bright flash shot from Suzanne's weapon, Neil came back into the room where Molly and Julio were being held.

"Come with me," Neil ordered the frightened pair.

Molly was numb with fear. "Is Peter dead?" she asked in a shaky voice.

"Of course not," Neil responded. "Why would we destroy a perfectly good human specimen? He was becoming overexcited, so Suzanne just erased part of his short-term memory."

Neil turned around and pointed to the screens to show that Peter was still alive.

Julio knew this was their only chance. He leapt up and knocked Neil hard on the head with the remote control. The Vandroid collapsed to the floor and Julio and Molly jumped past him out into the corridor. The door slammed shut behind them, locking Neil inside.

"What do we do now?" asked Molly. "Without our masks, the first Vandroid we meet will recognize us and turn us in!"

"Remember what Suzanne said about our replicas?" asked Julio as he ran down the corridor looking for the greenhouse room.

"Yeah, so what?" Molly replied as she ran beside him.

"Well, if we run into any Vandroids, just pretend you are your own replica," suggested Julio. "Say only what you said in the sound booth."

The two teens slowed to a walk. They removed their jumpsuits from over their own clothes to avoid attracting attention.

More and more Vandroids were now coming into the spaceship as Julio and Molly searched for the room where Peter was being held captive.

"They're all coming back in from the lot," said Julio to Molly. "They must be getting ready to take off."

"We've got to hurry!" Molly said, starting to walk faster. She was so tense even the sight of her own reflection in the shiny surface of the corridor made her jump.

Molly jumped again when she

thought she saw yet another mirror. She stopped short. Julio did the same. They looked at each other. Then they looked back at themselves—exact Vandroid replicas of themselves!

CHAPTER EIGHT

"Who are you?" asked Molly.

"My name is Molly Eng. I am sixteen years old," said the replica who stood facing her in the corridor.

Peter's replica stood there, too, next to Julio's replica.

"If only this were the real Peter, we could get out of here now!" Julio whispered to Molly.

"I have an idea," Molly whispered back. "You find Peter, I'll get rid of these three replicas."

"How?" asked Julio.

She quickly told him her plan.

Julio shrugged and kept walking. Molly remained facing the replicas.

"Would you like to play a game?" Molly asked them.

All three replicas nodded their heads at once. They had obviously been programmed to like games.

"Okay," Molly continued. "This game is called hide-and-seek. I'll close my eyes and count to ten. You three hurry and hide somewhere where no one can

see you. Then I'll come looking for you. You must stay in your hiding places until I find you. Okay?" Molly hoped the replicas understood the rules. Otherwise her plan wouldn't work.

All three Vandroid replicas enthusiastically nodded their heads in agreement.

Molly covered her eyes with her hands and peeked through her fingers as the replicas scattered to find perfect hiding places.

Just when the replicas had disappeared out of sight, Molly saw Suzanne walking toward her. She recognized the Vandroid by the gold dress.

"There you are," said Suzanne. "It's time for you to go home. Do you know where you live?"

Molly realized that Suzanne thought she was speaking to Molly's replica. Molly recited her address just as she had said it in the booth.

"Good," said Suzanne. "Now, where
are your friends?"

Just then Julio and Peter walked up.
"My name is Julio Cruz," Julio said in a
flat voice. He held Peter's arm tightly.

"Good, Julio," said Suzanne.

Molly couldn't believe Suzanne was
falling for their trick!

"Okay, you perfect Vandroid-made

models," said Suzanne as she led them to the exit. "Goodbye and good luck!"

The floor opened at their feet and three poles shot down from the spaceship to the ground below. Molly, Julio, and Peter quickly slid down.

Their feet hit the ground and they were off and running, Julio pulling Peter along by the hand. As they ran, the teens heard Neil's voice from inside the spaceship. "Wait! Those are not the replicas! Stop those Earthlings!"

But the poles had already retracted back into the spaceship. Panels were closing over the openings.

"Keep running!" shouted Molly to her friends as the three raced away from the spaceship.

Dozens of mice and rabbits were scrambling in all directions. Molly was thankful that the animals had escaped from the spaceship as well.

The three teens heard a rumbling and turned to see the spaceship lift off from the ground. Julio and Molly watched the spaceship vanish into the sky.

"Wow," said Molly. "That was close!" She turned to Julio. He was staring up where the spaceship had been hovering just seconds ago.

"Do you really think the replicas would have fooled our family and friends?" she asked him.

"My name is Julio Cruz. I am sixteen years old," Julio said in a flat voice.

Molly gasped in terror. "Julio?"

"Just kidding," Julio laughed. "But I think Peter's still pretty dazed."

"Are you all right?" Molly asked Peter. He was sitting down on the grass with his head in his hands.

"What happened?" Peter asked.

"We just escaped from a spaceship. Vandroids were going to take us to Vandra and put us in a zoo!" said Molly.

Peter laughed. "That's pretty original, Molly. But don't you think it would make a better movie if they just tried to

conquer Earth instead?"

"What movie?" asked Molly.

"There was no movie," added Julio.

Peter looked puzzled. "Isn't that why we're here? To try out for some science fiction movie?"

"You really don't remember *anything* about what just happened?" Julio asked.

"Of course I remember," Peter shot back. "We got up at the crack of dawn and hiked across town to try out for this movie. But there's nothing here, so I guess the flyer was some kind of stupid prank, huh?"

Molly and Julio looked at each other. Obviously Peter's memory of the past few hours had been completely erased.

"Come on," Peter urged. "Let's get something to eat. I'm starving. Then maybe we can go to a *real* movie downtown."

"Shouldn't we tell someone about what really happened?" Molly asked Julio.

"No one would believe us," said Julio. "Peter doesn't remember anything about the Vandroids. And the Vandroids were careful not to leave any traces behind."

"But what if the Vandroids come back?" asked Molly.

"After all that trouble they went through just to try to get three teenagers, I think they've learned it might not be worth it," said Julio.